All's RIGHT WITH the WORLD

Jennifer Adams Christopher Silas Neal

BALZER + BRAY
An Imprint of HarperCollinsPublishers

Balzer + Bray is an imprint of HarperCollins Publishers.

All's Right with the World
Text copyright © 2023 by Jennifer Adams
Illustrations copyright © 2023 by Christopher Silas Neal
All rights reserved. Manufactured in Italy.
No part of this book may be used or reproduced in any manner
whatsoever without written permission except in the case of brief
quotations embodied in critical articles and reviews. For information
address HarperCollins Children's Books, a division of
HarperCollins Publishers, 195 Broadway, New York, NY 10007.
www.harpercollinschildrens.com

Library of Congress Control Number: 2022931758
ISBN 978-0-06-296248-5

The artist used mixed media to create the illustrations for this book.
Typography by Dana Fritts. Hand lettering by Christopher Silas Neal.
22 23 24 25 26   RTLO   10 9 8 7 6 5 4 3 2 1
❖
First Edition

For Bill. Robert to my Elizabeth.

—J. A.

For Brooklyn.

— C. S. N.

The year's at the spring,
and day's at the morn.

Morning's at seven.

All's right with the world.

Waffles with berries,
umbrella, red tulips.

We set out for school.
All's right with the world.

Afternoon ramble.
The clouds in the sky.

The lark's on the wing.
The snail's on the thorn.

Scooters and skateboards.

Boots splashing in puddles.

Tag, hide-and-seek.

All's right with the world.

Warm bath, fluffy towel,

and notebooks and crayons.

The sun's going down.
The hill-side's dew-pearl'd.

The food's in the oven.

Plates on the table.

We hold hands in thanks.

All's right with the world.

Bedtime's at eight.
Cozy chair, favorite book.
Pajamas and pillows.

Good night to the world.

Robert Browning was born on May 7, 1812. He was a famous poet in the Victorian era. He was married to Elizabeth Barrett Browning, another famous poet.

Pippa's Song
By Robert Browning

The year's at the spring,

And day's at the morn;

Morning's at seven;

The hill-side's dew-pearl'd;

The lark's on the wing;

The snail's on the thorn;

God's in His heaven—

All's right with the world!